KASIA'S SURPRISE

STELLA GURNEY

Niamh

ILLUSTRATED BY

PETR HORÁČEK

WALKER
BOOKS

For my lovely boy Sam
S.G.

For Cecilia, thank you for your drawings
and inspiration
Daddy (P.H.)

*Many thanks to our Polish advisory committee, the pupils
of St Mary Magdalen's Catholic School in Brockley,
London, for all their help and suggestions*

First published 2010 by Walker Books Ltd
87 Vauxhall Walk, London SE11 5HJ

4 6 8 10 9 7 5 3

Text © 2010 Stella Gurney
Illustrations © 2010 Petr Horáček

This book has been typeset in Bembo Educational
and WBHoracek

Printed and bound in China

British Library Cataloguing in Publication Data:
a catalogue record for this book is available from the British Library

ISBN 978-1-4063-2331-3

www.walker.co.uk
www.petrhoracek.co.uk

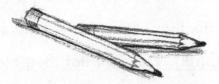

A few of the words in this story are Polish, which is the language spoken by Kasia and her family. This is what they mean and how you say them:

babcia [bab-cha]: grandmother
dziadek [ja-dek]: grandfather
Glowa do góry! [gwo-va do goo-rry]: Cheer up!
Kasia, aniele [Kash-a, an-yell-e]: Kasia, my angel
misiu [mee-su]: teddy bear
pierogi [peer-og-ee]: filled dumplings
slonko [swon-ko]: little sunshine

NAMES
Kasia Nowak [Kash-a No-vak]
Agnieszka [Ag-nyes-ka] (Kasia's mum)
Jan [Yan] (Kasia's grandpa)
Wisła Kraków [Vees-wa Krak-uf] (Polish football team from the city of Kraków)

Kasia Sends a Letter

"Well done, everyone," called Mrs
Hughes over the sudden noise. The end
of day bell had sounded and children
were bouncing and clambering in their
chairs, chatting excitedly. "Home time!
I hope you have wonderful holidays –
I know Mr Carlson will want to hear
all about them when you come back."

It was the last day of school before the summer break. Kasia watched as Daisy, Saraya and Daria ran to hug Mrs Hughes and ask her to sign their reading books. Daisy the Drip was even crying! When they came back in September, the class would have a new teacher, Mr Carlson.

Mrs Hughes was kind, funny
and nice. Mr Carlson was kind of
funny-*looking* and – from what Kasia
had seen of him on playground duty –
not very nice.

The last day of school wasn't really like school at all. For a start, you could wear what you wanted. A few children had dressed up as fairies or superheroes. Kasia was wearing the Wisła Kraków football shirt her dziadek had bought her, although it was a bit small now.

Some children had brought
in little presents for the
teacher. Mum had asked
Kasia if she wanted to
take something, but Kasia
had said no, even though she
really liked Mrs Hughes.

In the afternoon everyone had
helped take down the colourful work
displays from the classroom walls
to make it ready for next year.

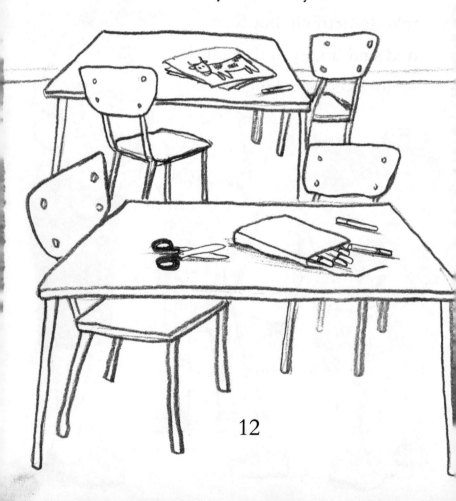

Now the room was empty and bare. Kasia thought it looked a bit like the flat she lived in with Mum.

Kasia didn't call their flat "home" –
that was back in Poland, in their
little town near the mountains, where
Babcia and Dziadek lived just
round the corner.

Kasia and her mum had left Poland to move to England after Christmas. Kasia missed so many things – her language, her school, her friends. But most of all she missed her babcia and dziadek. She didn't like England *at all*. She'd known she wouldn't, and she hadn't changed her mind. She wished Mum hadn't brought her here.

The group around Mrs Hughes got bigger. Kasia thought about joining it, but then she decided not to. She picked up her bag and headed for the door.

"Kasia!" called a voice from the other side of the classroom.

She turned to see Kyle, sitting on some desks in the corner with Tom and Kamil.

"I like your shirt!" he said.

His friends laughed.

Was he teasing her? Kasia frowned
and hurried out of the classroom,
red-faced.

17

"There you are!" said Mum as
Kasia came through the doors into
the hotel foyer. "Isn't it hot today!
How was school?"

"All right,"
said Kasia.
"Hi, Jim."

"Hello, love," said Jim, and waved. Jim worked on reception with Mum at the hotel; Kasia always walked there after school and waited for her mum to finish work. Sometimes Kasia would sit in the room behind the big reception desk and do her homework.

Other times, Kasia would
wander around the foyer and
pretend she was one of the
guests. She liked listening
to people's conversations.

Once, Kasia overheard an
old lady say to her husband,
"Before we go, Frank, have you been?"

"Been? Been where, dear? How can
I have been before we've even gone?"
asked her husband
innocently.
He caught
Kasia's eye
and winked
at her.

20

"*You* know, Frank," said the old lady. "Have you *been*?"

The man carried on pretending he didn't understand, until in the end his wife was forced to say, "Have you been TO THE TOILET?" very loudly.

Everyone turned and stared and she went bright red. Kasia wondered why she hadn't just said that in the first place. English people were very strange sometimes.

21

Today Kasia sat in the little staffroom behind reception. She was writing a letter to Babcia and Dziadek.

Dear D & B,

How are you? I hope you are well. I miss you very much. I wish I was at home with you. The summer holidays started today. Mum says she will take some days off and we can do things together. On the other days I'll go to the holiday club. I don't want to – it sounds rubbish. We're going to go to Ikea to buy some things to make the flat more cosy but I don't think it will ever be as cosy as our house at home. I wish I could see you. Sorry this letter is so short.

Lots and lots and lots of love,

Kasia xoxoxoxoxoxox

PS Did you go to the match last Saturday?

On the way home that evening, Kasia and Mum posted the letter. In England postboxes were tall and round. At home they were small and square … Kasia even missed Polish postboxes!

That night, as she fell asleep, she imagined she was the letter, flying through the sky all the way home to Poland and arriving, safe and sound, at her babcia and dziadek's house.

Kasia Receives a Letter

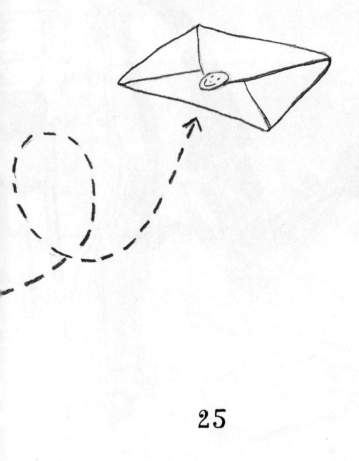

"Jan, look!" called Babcia. "The post's just arrived – there's a letter from Kasia!"

Kasia's grandfather pushed the front door shut behind him with his foot and put down his shopping bags, listening as his wife read it out.

"Poor little thing," sighed Babcia when she'd finished. "She sounds so homesick."

"She's all right," grunted Dziadek. "You know Kasia. She wouldn't enjoy *Disney*land if she was forced to go."

Babcia smiled. "True, the little madam. Do you remember that time she sulked because she wasn't allowed to wear her pink shoes? You promised her a strawberry ice cream if she would give you a smile, and you were tickling her and she was wriggling all over the place but she *still* wouldn't smile? She's stubborn, that one."

"I bought her an ice cream anyway."

"You did, you big *misiu*. Still, it must be very difficult for her over there. New country, new language. It's a lot for a young girl. I can't wait to see her again. Did you remember to print off the airline tickets?"

"Of course. And look what I bought to wear when we get there!" Dziadek fished an enormous T-shirt out of a shopping bag and held it up against himself, waggling his hips. It had a big red double-decker bus on the front.

"I got you one too."

"Ooh!" said Babcia, clapping her hands. "We'll fit right in!"

Kasia's grandmother bustled back
into the kitchen to sort out lunch while
Dziadek settled down with the TV
remote. He chuckled to himself at the
thought that in a few days they would
be flying to the UK for three weeks to
see their beloved Kasia. And it was a
secret – she had no idea! He couldn't
wait to see the look on her face
when she saw them.

That evening, after dinner,
Babcia cleared away the dishes
and washed up, then she got out
the writing paper while Dziadek
sat in his favourite armchair
to let his meal go down.

"Right!" said Babcia. "What shall we say?"

Dziadek thought for a moment and then said,

"Dear Kasia."

Babcia's pen began scratching over the page as Dziadek continued.

"Sorry you're not enjoying England. We know how hard it must be for you. At least the holidays are here now and you don't have to go to school. Babcia and I have a holiday coming up too. We're going to visit someone we're both very fond of. It's supposed to be quite rainy where they live, so we're packing our waterproofs."

34

"We can't say that," said Babcia, looking up. "She'll guess!"

"She won't," chuckled Dziadek. He carried on.

We'll be there for a few weeks, so you won't get any letters for a while. Still, I'm sure things won't seem so bad soon. Głowa do góry! Lots of love and kisses, Babcia and Dziadek.

"Ooh – add this bit too," said Dziadek.

PS Of course I went last Saturday – but the lads aren't playing well. I think they're missing their best supporter! Dziadek.

"Lovely!" said Babcia, licking and sealing the envelope. "I'll walk to the end of the road and post it right away. Oh, I do love a surprise! I can't wait to see little Kasia's face when she realizes we've come to visit *her*! Hee hee!"

Kasia's Surprise

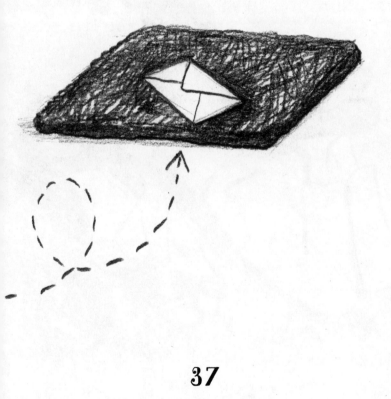

Kasia was fed up. She was sitting in
the hotel staffroom again. Her mum
had only had one day off work so far,
and she'd been too tired to go to Ikea.
Instead they'd gone to the park
and lain in the sunshine.
Kasia had actually
quite enjoyed
herself, but she
hadn't let Mum
know that.

She sighed. Then sighed again, more loudly this time. Mum still didn't hear her – she was busy on reception.

Kasia wished she wasn't so grumpy all the time. She knew Mum was doing her best, but why couldn't they have just stayed in Poland with all her friends?

And now Babcia and Dziadek had written to say they were off on a long trip. Kasia wouldn't even get letters from them! It was *so* unfair. Her throat suddenly felt sore as tears rose up.

Just then, Mum called from reception, "Kasia! Can you come here, please?" Her voice sounded funny and high. Kasia blinked quickly and hurried through. Mum probably needed her to run an errand. She didn't usually look so happy about it, though. She had a huge, excited grin on her face. What was the matter with her?

Behind a tall potted plant, Kasia
could see the tops of two people's
heads: a man's and a woman's. The
woman's hair was dyed dark red, a bit
like Babcia's. And the man had
a big shiny bald patch,
a bit like…

DZIADEK?

Kasia gave a little scream and ran round the desk. There they were – her lovely babcia and dziadek, holding out their arms to her and laughing.

It was so strange to see them there! Kasia almost couldn't believe they were real, until she threw herself into their hugs. Solid, cuddly, warm: they *were* real! Her babcia and dziadek were really, really here!

"Did you know?" Kasia asked finally, turning to Mum.

"Of course!" laughed Mum, tears shining in her eyes. "We've been planning it for months!"

Kasia thought she had never felt
so happy.

Mum finished work then, and
they took Babcia and Dziadek
back to the flat.

Mum had made *pierogi* for tea,
and afterwards they sat about talking
and laughing.

"Kasia's doing so well at school,"
Mum said proudly. "Tell them that
poem you learned, *slonko*."

Kasia felt shy, but she stood up
and recited the poem
they had done
in class.

"That was great!" clapped Dziadek
when she had finished.

"Doesn't she speak English well,"
whispered Babcia loudly to Mum.
Kasia blushed and wriggled, but
secretly she was pleased.

First thing the next morning, Kasia
ran into the front room, where
Babcia and Dziadek were
snoring on the fold-out sofa.

"Mum says, do you want a cup of tea?" Kasia asked, shaking Dziadek.

"Well, now we *really* know we're in England," he grunted, opening one eye. "Go on, then. I'll need to wear my English outfit today – have a look in my bag. There's a new T-shirt near the top."

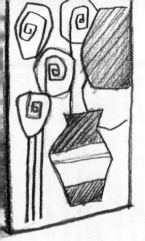

Kasia pulled out the T-shirt
with the big red bus on and
giggled to herself. "It's lovely,
Dziadek!" She grinned.
"Exactly what everyone
wears here."

After breakfast
Mum had to go to work.

"Kasia, *aniele*," said Babcia,
"why don't you take us out and show
us around?"

It was another beautiful day.
The pavement was hot under Kasia's
flip-flops.

"That's my school," she said,
pointing it out to her grandparents.
It felt strange and quiet without any
children shouting in the playground.
Kasia almost felt sorry for it.

"And there's our church," she said
a little further on. "The priest's quite
funny. We go to him for Polish school.

"That's where we sometimes do our washing – but I like the other launderette better; you can get rainbow drops in the shop next door.

And here's the Polish shop. But you should try baked beans and Marmite while you're here – they're really nice!"

Babcia and Dziadek
exchanged a smile. Their little
Kasia didn't seem like someone
who hated where she lived.

"I'll take you back through the
park," Kasia chatted on. "It's got
a really cool play area."

The sun shone through patches in the leafy trees in the park. Families sat on blankets in the shade with picnics. Kasia licked the ice cream Dziadek had bought her and then handed it to him to hold.

Behind the play area
some children were playing
football.

"Look at me!" called Kasia, hanging
upside down from the top of the
climbing frame. Dziadek laughed
and waved, taking a big lick of her
ice cream.

"Kasia!" came a shout.

A boy wearing the Wisła Kraków team strip came running over. It was Kyle. He grinned, pointing at his shirt. "Told you I liked them!" he said. "Hey, do you want to play footie with us? We need someone in goal."

"I've got my grandparents here,"
said Kasia awkwardly.

"Great team, son!" Dziadek
called over.

Kyle laughed and gave him
a thumbs up. "Maybe another
day, then?" he said to Kasia.

"Yeah. OK," she replied.

"Bye," called Kyle as he ran
back to the game.

Kasia climbed down and went to get her ice cream back.

"Kasia Nowak," said Dziadek, smiling at her, "I think you like it here a lot more than you let on."

Kasia made a face. "Maybe," she shrugged, and then let out a shriek as Dziadek caught her up in his arms and began to tickle her. "OK," she giggled. "I like it here! I do. I do! I DO!"

Dear D & B,

I miss you so much! Thank you for coming. I loved it. Mum did too. Here's a picture of all of us when we went to the zoo. I am going to play in the park now with Kyle and Janek and Tom and Saraya. It is still really really REALLY hot!

Miss you loads and loads and loads.

Kasia xxxxxxxxxxxxxxxxxxxxxxxx